# The Barefoot Book of
# Earth Tales

retold by
## Dawn Casey

illustrated by
## Anne Wilson

Barefoot Books
*Step inside a story*

# Introduction

Whether we live in the city or in the country, we depend on the Earth in all kinds of ways: we need to use its materials for shelter and for clothes; we must have clean water to drink; and we rely on successful harvests to eat. We may sometimes think of ourselves as separate from nature, but in fact the cycle of our lives is completely interwoven with the cycles of the natural world.

Traditionally, people have lived very close to nature, enjoying the gifts she has to offer and being respectful in turn. The stories from these cultures reflect this: the oldest tales tell of Earth Mothers and World Trees, Ancient Oceans and Heavenly Gardens. They tell of wonderful spirits and talking animals. Many religions and faiths teach that the heavenly reveals itself through nature. All over the world, songs and stories express a deep understanding of the Earth as sacred.

Sadly, this respect for nature is not as strong as it was even a hundred years ago. Recently, many people and institutions have begun to take a more selfish approach to the natural world — as something to use and make money out of, without caring about the damage that their actions may cause.

Now, at a time when we are again becoming aware that we need to live in balance with our planet, these ancient stories offer an important message. I have chosen a selection of tales that both celebrate our connection with nature, and remind us how important it is to look after this Earth, our home. There are myths to renew our understanding of the land, stories that celebrate the glory and beauty of the natural world, and wisdom tales about how to care for the Earth.

Listening to these ancient stories today and acting on their advice helps us to move forward, as the caretakers of tomorrow.

Dawn Casey, Lewes, Britain, 2009

# Contents

# Australia

There are many different groups of indigenous, or native, peoples living in Australia, each with their own particular language and culture. Common to all these peoples is the concept of 'the Dreaming' and a belief that the Earth and all living things are sacred.

The Dreaming stories tell of ancestral spirit-beings. At the beginning of the world, the ancestors travelled across the land creating mountains, rivers and deserts, kangaroos and honey-ants: they created every feature and creature of the Earth.

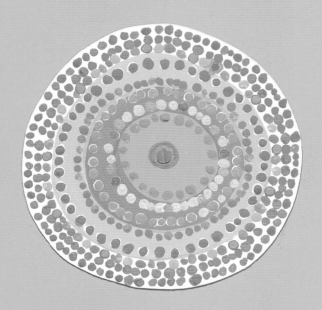

To Aboriginal Australians, the spirits of the ancestors are still present everywhere, and in every living thing. These spirits still inhabit the rocks, plants, animals, stars, wind and rain today, watching over their creations. Because the Earth is alive with these spirits, all of nature is sacred.

Each person belongs to and is a guardian of the place of their birth. They have special responsibilities to protect and preserve the spirit of the land and the life forms that are a part of it.

People go on journeys (called walkabouts) to tend to their own birthplace and those of their ancestors. They perform ceremonies and rituals, re-enacting the Dreaming in paintings, dances, story and song.

If each one of us looks after that little patch of earth where we belong, between us we can care for the whole Earth.

# The Sun Mother

## AUSTRALIA

In the long ago, in the time before time, there was darkness. There was silence. The Earth was asleep. Under the surface of the land, all the forms of life lay sleeping.

Up in the sky, the Sun Mother was also asleep.

Until one day she heard the Great Spirit whisper, 'Wake up, my child.' The Sun Mother inhaled deeply and the still air vibrated. She opened her eyes and light washed over the world.

The Great Spirit spoke again. 'It is time for you to wake the Earth.' The Sun Mother smiled a sunbeam smile, and the Earth was warmed.

Swift as a shooting star, she flew down to the empty Earth. The ground was cold and hard beneath her feet. Very gently, she took a step. And as her bare foot touched the bare soil, she felt a wonderful sensation and wiggled her toes. She lifted her foot, and the first green shoots of grass on the planet were revealed. With each step she took, fresh green grass sprang up in her footprints.

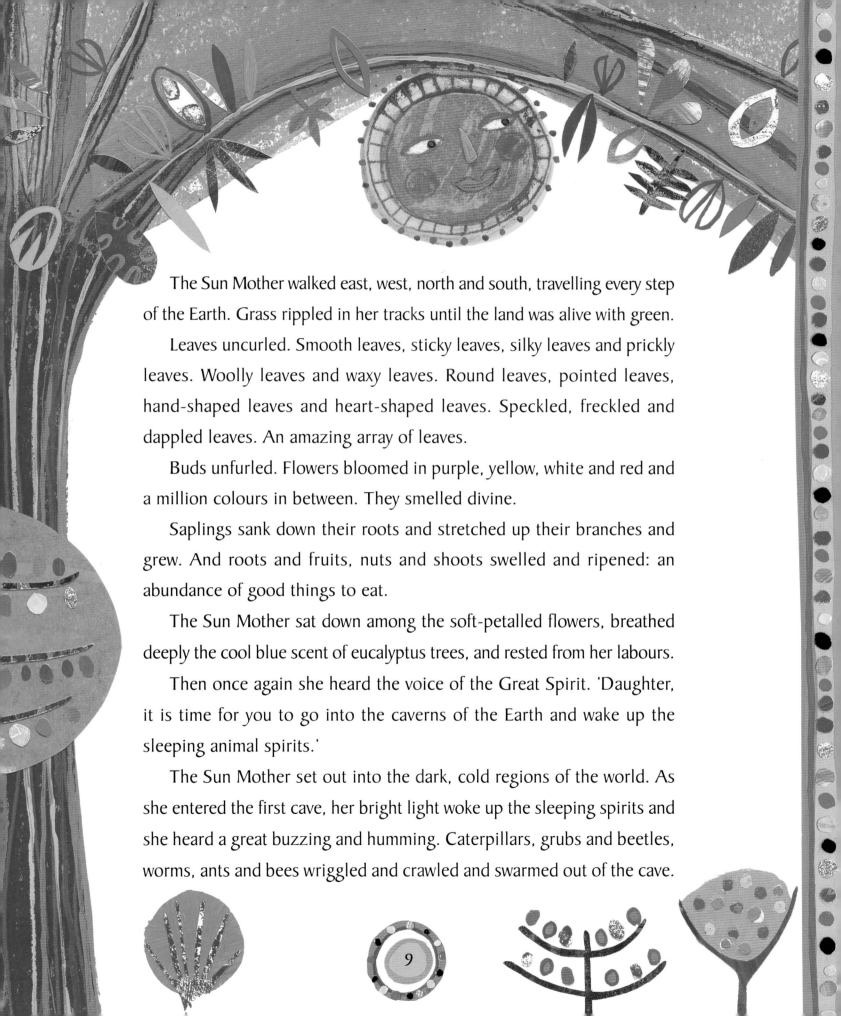

The Sun Mother walked east, west, north and south, travelling every step of the Earth. Grass rippled in her tracks until the land was alive with green.

Leaves uncurled. Smooth leaves, sticky leaves, silky leaves and prickly leaves. Woolly leaves and waxy leaves. Round leaves, pointed leaves, hand-shaped leaves and heart-shaped leaves. Speckled, freckled and dappled leaves. An amazing array of leaves.

Buds unfurled. Flowers bloomed in purple, yellow, white and red and a million colours in between. They smelled divine.

Saplings sank down their roots and stretched up their branches and grew. And roots and fruits, nuts and shoots swelled and ripened: an abundance of good things to eat.

The Sun Mother sat down among the soft-petalled flowers, breathed deeply the cool blue scent of eucalyptus trees, and rested from her labours.

Then once again she heard the voice of the Great Spirit. 'Daughter, it is time for you to go into the caverns of the Earth and wake up the sleeping animal spirits.'

The Sun Mother set out into the dark, cold regions of the world. As she entered the first cave, her bright light woke up the sleeping spirits and she heard a great buzzing and humming. Caterpillars, grubs and beetles, worms, ants and bees wriggled and crawled and swarmed out of the cave.

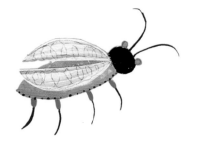

When the Sun Mother walked out into the world again, she was leading a kaleidoscope of butterflies behind her. The insects flitted and fluttered from bush to bush, and the world was a dance of shimmering colour.

Again, the Sun Mother rested. She looked down from the mountaintops at the splendour of the Earth, and beamed with delight.

Refreshed, the Sun Mother walked down, down, down, into the next cave. She stepped down onto solid ice. With the touch of her foot, the ice began to melt and squeeze between her toes. Beneath her feet a stream started to flow, splashing around her ankles. Her warmth woke up lizards, frogs and snakes. A river gurgled out of the cavern, filling up lakes and lagoons, creeks and billabongs, and the deep wide sea.

The Sun Mother walked out into the world once again, trailing her fingertips through the rippling waters. All around her swam seahorses and turtles, and fish of every size and every shade from pearly silver to coral red.

Again the Sun Mother rested, for she was filled to the brim with the wonder of the world.

When the Sun Mother went into the coldest, darkest cave, in the deepest loins of the Earth, she was accompanied by a procession of crawling creatures, some wriggling their way on hundreds of legs and others slithering on no legs at all.

She looked down into the depths of the cavern, and her face shone with love. All along the ledges were the spirit forms of birds and animals. Her presence woke up the feathered tribes and the furry clans. With a flutter and clatter of wings, birds of every call and cry burst out of the cave and into existence.

Parrots whistled, emus waddled and the treetops rang with the laughter of kookaburras. Then out came the animals. An infinite variety; a jubilant hullabaloo.

All the creatures gathered around the Sun Mother, glad to be alive. The Sun Mother spoke softly to the multitude of beings assembled around her. 'Listen, my children. Like seeds in the winter, you slept in the earth. Like seeds in the spring, I have woken you. Now my work is complete, and I shall return to my home in the sky. Now I must leave you.'

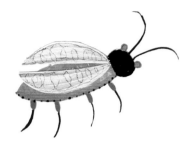

Suddenly, in a ball of light, the Sun Mother soared up high into the western sky. All the creatures watched with fearful eyes as the Earth became darker and darker. When the Sun Mother disappeared over the rim of the world, they cried and howled like babies left alone in the night.

As the darkness deepened and the Sun Mother still did not return, the crying died down. Everything was silent. Nothing moved. Eventually, the creatures rested.

One tiny bird, a wagtail, kept on looking, kept on listening, always alert. On the eastern horizon she saw faint but growing brighter, the first rays of dawn. She hopped up and down, calling out her message for all to hear: 'The Sun Mother has returned!'

One by one, each and every bird joined in her song, singing out their joy to the world. Each and every creature watched the skies, and the first sunrise lit up their eyes.

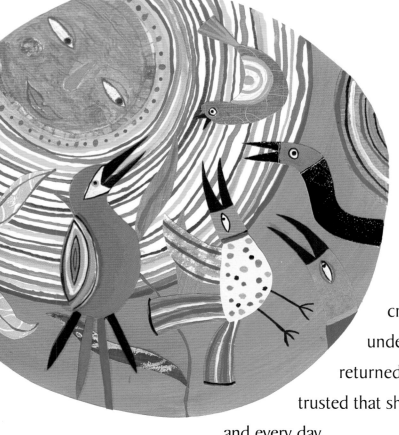

But the Sun Mother did not return to the Earth. She continued her journey across the whole wide arc of the sky, to the west. Again the world was dark, but this time the creatures were not afraid. They understood that the Sun Mother had returned to her home in the sky and they trusted that she would come back to visit them each and every day.

And so the rhythm of the day came into being, from dew-sparkled dawn through long, glorious hours and into a sunset, blazing copper and scarlet and gold. And night followed day in a never-ending cycle.

Many dawns and many sunsets came and went. Time passed. The creatures forgot the joy they had first felt, basking in the Sun Mother's warmth. Day after day, they forgot how lucky they were to be alive among the whole of creation.

Fish gazed at the sunshine glittering on the surface of their ponds and longed to feel its play upon their skin and to explore the world above. Furry animals longed to feel the cool of the pool and to explore the watery depths. 'I want to swoop and soar like a bird,' cried a tiny mouse. Their loud complaints reached the home of the Sun Mother.

Swift as a shooting star, the Sun Mother returned to Earth and gathered her people around her. 'Children,' she said gently, 'I want you to be content. If you are unhappy with your shape, I will give you a chance to change it. Choose carefully, for the form you take now will be yours for a long time.'

That is how some mice sprouted wings and flapped into the sky as bats, and certain furry land dwellers slipped into the sea as seals. Certain insects were even granted their wish to look like twigs and leaves.

The Earth was a harmony of beings, in every form imaginable, and some beyond imagining! With so many marvels to choose from, Platypus wanted a beak like Duck, fur like Kangaroo *and* soft-shelled eggs like Lizard.

When all the creatures were content with their forms, the Sun Mother said, 'Now I will send you something new: I will give you a part of myself, to light up the night.'

The next morning, when the animal tribes awoke, they saw a luminous

being rising out of the eastern sky. 'This is Morning Star,' the Sun Mother told her children. 'He is a son of the spirit world; he is one of you. Tonight at twilight, watch the western sky, and I will send you a daughter too.'

That night, Moon rose. And so, the cycle of day and night was complete. During the day, the Sun Mother beamed and gleamed. At night, the world was bathed in moonlight.

From their sky home, Morning Star and Moon looked down to the Earth, where the birds were building their nests and all the creatures were living and loving with their companions and their young.

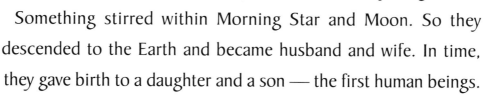

Something stirred within Morning Star and Moon. So they descended to the Earth and became husband and wife. In time, they gave birth to a daughter and a son — the first human beings.

'Welcome!' the Sun Mother said to the first people of the Earth. And when she spoke, her words brightened the air.

'Look around you — this is the place you belong to. All around you are your family: the land, the wind and the waters, the plants and the animals. You are all part of the same spirit.

'I have walked every step of the Earth and now it is awake. The Earth is alive. The Earth is sacred.

'Care for creation. Look after the land for your ancestors; look after the land for your children and for your children's children.'

With these words, the Sun Mother soared up into the sky and smiled down on the newly awoken world.

The Earth was alive with green. It was bright with flowers. It danced with movement. Fish of every size and

shape swam in the deep oceans and clear rivers. Creatures of every colour and kind crept and crawled, hung and swung, slithered and fluttered and hopped in trees and mountains and swamps. Birds of every call and cry filled the air with music.

And people tried their best to care for creation.

It was a beautiful world. It still is.

# Make a song-line painting

Paint an Aboriginal-style picture of a place that is special to you.

You will need:
- Paints (Traditional Aboriginal pigments came from the earth: sand yellow and red-brown from ochre, white from clay and black from charcoal. Use these colours or choose colours that reflect the place you belong to)
- Something for printing dots: cotton ball, pencil or finger!
- Paint brushes
- Drawing paper, brown paper or canvas

**Step 1:** Traditional Aboriginal art shows areas that have special meaning to people.

Choose a place or a journey that has special meaning for you, such as a campsite in the woods or a walk through the park.

**Step 2:** Like a map, Aboriginal pictures often show how the land looks from above. Look at the key then invent your own symbols.

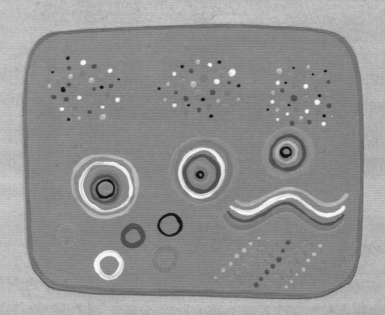

Dots — Trees
Concentric Circles — Camp
Curved Lines — Rivers
Circles — Rocks
Group of Dots — Smoke or Rain

**Step 3:** Aboriginal pictures recount the journeys of people and animals by showing the marks they made on the ground as they travelled. A person's journey might be shown by a straight line or footprints. A squiggly line could be a snake, while a trail of paw prints could show a dog walking.

Paint the route of animals and people into your picture.

**Step 4:** For the background, dip your finger into the paint and dab the colour onto your paper. Fill the spaces in your picture until the whole surface is covered with dots, lines and patterns.

# Nigeria

This folk tale comes from the Edo people of Nigeria. In the thirteenth century, the Edo founded the Kingdom of Benin, deep in the West African rainforest.

The kingdom was well known for its arts. Artisans and craftspeople fashioned terracotta sculptures, bronze statues and wooden masks.

Musicians and storytellers enthralled and entertained. In the evening, people would gather together to listen to the storytellers' tales.

Like many African myths, this tale tells how humans once lived closer and in harmony with nature. It also shows how our own actions have the power to create or destroy this balance. The story is hundreds of years old, yet it offers a timely reminder to consume less and conserve more.

As Gandhi said, 'The Earth can provide for every man's need, but not for every man's greed.'

Without meaning to, we often take more than we need. About one fourth of the food we buy ends up being thrown in the rubbish bin.

Production, transportation and storage use a lot of energy, water and packaging, which is all wasted if the food is thrown away uneaten.

At the moment, most of our edible waste is sent to landfill sites, where it gives off harmful greenhouse gases that contribute to climate change and pollution.

If we stop wasting food that could be eaten, we could feed 80 million people a day.

# Why the Sky Is Far Away
## NIGERIA

A story is coming. Stop talking and listen. In the beginning, the sky was close to the Earth. So close you could reach up and touch it. And you could eat it! In those days, people always had enough to eat, without ever having to work for it. Men and women did not have to plough the fields and sow the seeds and gather the crops. Children did not have to fetch sticks for the fire. Whenever anybody was hungry, they just reached up and tore off a piece of sky.

But people grew careless with the sky's gifts. They broke off more sky than they needed. After all, the sky was so big; there would always be enough for everybody. Who cared about a little wasted sky?

22

But the sky cared. Soon the sky's sorrow turned to resentment, and its resentment grew to anger. 'I offer myself every day to these people,' the sky brooded, 'and they throw me away, half eaten, like rubbish.'

'People of Earth!' The sky's eyes flashed like lightning. Clouds bubbled and boiled. 'You have not treated me with respect. You have wasted my gifts.'

Trembling, the people looked up.

'I warn you. If you are greedy, I will leave. I will move far away.'

With lowered eyes, the people listened. On bended knees, they promised to be more careful.

After that, no one broke off more than they could eat. And they always remembered to thank the sky.

But then the time came for the greatest festival of the year, in honour of the chief of the kingdom. The night rang with music. Bells clanged and drums banged. People stamped and clapped and laughed.

Palm wine flowed. The tables heaved with dishes of specially prepared sky. Sky cut and shaped, sky moulded and sculpted, sky in every flavour, from custard apple to coco plum. There was plenty for everyone, for the sky was generous. It trusted people to take only what they needed.

But there was one woman who was never satisfied. Osato always wanted more. Her arms were heavy with brass bracelets. But brass wasn't good enough for her — she wanted coral beads. She dressed in robes of the finest cotton. But she wanted red silk. And most of all, she loved to eat.

First she helped herself to a handful of noon-yellow sky. Mmm — sticky-sweet pineapple. Chunk after chunk disappeared into her mouth. Then she ladled out some sky stew, spicy and warm. Oh, that was good! She lifted the dish to her lips, draining it, dumplings and all. Soon her stomach was stuffed. Her neck was flushed. She loosened her robe. What next? Delicate slices of morning sky, pink and glistening. With a swift movement, she scooped them up and slurped them down all at once. Ahh — watermelon. Juice dribbled down her chin.

At last the tables were empty. Osato was full, so she waddled home.

Her robe stretched and strained around her stomach. And even though she was full to bursting, her eyes kept wandering upwards, towards the sky. What would it taste like right now? Citrus storms? Her taste buds tingled. Luscious mango? Her mouth watered. Honey sunsets? She licked her lips.

Her fingers began to pull out her spoon — the one she kept tucked in her headscarf — just in case. She stopped herself just in time. Osato knew that the sky offered itself only because no one ever took more than they needed. And she knew she didn't need any more. But oh, how she wanted some! Just one more spoonful.

She stared up, drooling. The sky was frothy white with clouds.

'The sky is so huge,' Osato told herself. 'It can't hurt to have just a little more.'

She pulled out her spoon and plunged it in. She savoured a mouthful of sky. And another. It tasted of golden pawpaw and coconut milk. It melted on her tongue. She closed her eyes. Oh! It tasted like floating in clouds. She threw down her spoon and scooped with her hands, sucking the delicious sky from her fingertips.

Finally, without another thought, Osato pulled down a great slab of sky. Enough to feed a family for weeks.

She licked all around the edges, chewing more slowly now. She stared up at the huge hole above her. She stared down at the enormous mound of sky. And she knew that she had taken more than even she could eat. Above her head, there were rumblings. 'What have I done?' Osato gasped. 'I cannot waste this sky. What shall I do?'

'Husband!' she shrieked. 'Come eat this sky.'

But her husband had been feasting too and was slumped in his chair, wafting himself with a fan. 'I can't even move, let alone eat!' Still, he managed a few mouthfuls.

'Children!' screeched Osato. Out ran Osato's children, chattering and giggling. They prodded the heap of sticky sky and screwed up their faces. Still, they forced down a few fingerfuls.

'Neighbours, please!' screamed Osato. 'Help me finish this sky.' Her neighbours had been at the festival too — at the sight of more food, they held their stomachs and groaned. But they ate as much as they could, with worried frowns on their faces and anxious glances above their heads.

But even with the help of the entire village, they could not eat that last piece of sky. Osato had taken too much. 'What does it matter?' Osato told herself at last. 'Just a bit of waste.' But the feeling in the pit of her stomach told her otherwise.

No one slept well that night. Osato lay staring into darkness.

The next morning, the sky did not offer his food to the people. Parents had nothing for breakfast. Children cried, hungry. Osato knelt on the ground, rocking and sobbing. 'I'm so sorry…'

But the sky just sighed. With a great rush of air, it lifted itself up. High as the treetops.

'I'm so sorry…' wept Osato.

High as the mountaintops.

'I'm so sorry…'

High above the Earth rose the sky, far beyond the reach of humans. 'I gave you all you needed,' its voice floated down to Osato, 'but still you took more. I cannot stand such greed. I must leave. I will not return.'

'But how will we live?' wept Osato. 'What will we eat?'

There was silence.

Osato's tears fell to the Earth. And the Earth spoke. 'Dry your tears,' it said gently. 'I can feed you. But you will have to work for your living. You will have to learn to plough fields and sow seeds and harvest crops. And remember what you have learned today. Take only what you need. And I will give it gladly.'

'Oh, I will,' promised Osato through her tears. 'I'll never take more than I need — never, ever again.'

Osato kept her word. She respected the sky, and the earth, and she shared her story with everyone around her. Now I have shared it with you.

# Make anything-goes soup

Use your leftovers with this simple recipe.

You will need:
- 500gms vegetables (Anything goes! Carrots, sweet potatoes, celery, broccoli, cauliflower, courgettes, sprouts, onions...)
- 1 litre broth (vegetable, chicken or beef)
- 1 x 200gm tin of chopped tomatoes
- $\frac{1}{2}$ tsp of chopped basil
- Salt and pepper to taste
- Grated Parmesan and crusty bread

**Step 1:** Chop the leftover vegetables and put them into a large saucepan.

**Step 2:** Add the broth and the chopped tomatoes.

**Step 3:** If you need more liquid, just add more broth or a tinned soup. Or, to make your soup more filling, add cooked kidney beans or cooked pasta.

**Step 4:** Season to taste, using the basil, salt and pepper.

**Step 5:** Simmer until cooked.

**Step 6:** Serve your anything-goes soup with grated Parmesan, crusty bread and a smile, knowing that nothing has gone to waste!

# American Southwest

**M**any different groups of native peoples live in North America. Traditionally, they share a similar understanding of humankind's relationship with the Earth.

In 1854, Chief Seathl, leader of a West Coast tribe, expressed this way of seeing the environment:

'Every shining pine needle, every clearing, every sandy shore, every mist in the dark woods and every humming insect is holy in the memory and experience of my people.

Teach your children what we have taught our children, that the Earth is our mother. The rivers are our brothers; they quench our thirst and feed our children. The air is precious to the red man, for all things share the same breath — the beast, the tree, the man — they all share the same breath.

This we know. The Earth does not belong to man: man belongs to the Earth. Man did not weave the web of life; he is merely a strand in it. Whatever he does to the web, he does to himself.'

The story of 'She Who Is Alone' comes from the Southern Plains of North America, land of the Comanche. It shows the value of giving to, rather than taking from, the Earth.

The beautiful blue flowers in this story still grow on the hills of the Southern Plains. The Comanche call the flower buffalo clover. When Europeans came to the country, they called the land Texas and the flower the bluebonnet.

# She Who Is Alone

## AMERICAN SOUTHWEST

No mother. No father. The famine had taken the girl's whole family. The people of the camp, the Comanche, cared for her and named her. They called her She Who Is Alone.

Since the famine, her only friend was her little buckskin doll. Her father had saved the softest hide to make the doll's body. Her mother had painted on the eyes and mouth with the juice of berries. With careful hands she had beaded the tiny leggings. Using her own hair, she had made long black plaits. The doll's plaits were tied with colourful scraps of cloth and decorated with a bright feather. A blue feather, butterfly blue.

She Who Is Alone loved her doll.

Every new spring moon, the Comanche people danced, singing and praying to the Great Spirit so the life-giving rains would come. In the shade of the tepees,

She Who Is Alone cradled her doll in her arms and watched the dancers as they dipped and pounded to the drum song.

But this year, the rains had not come. Plants wilted. Rivers dried up. The land cracked. Hunters returned without buffalo. Many people died.

So for three days, the people danced and drummed and sang: 'Great Spirit, the land is dying. Your people are dying. Tell us what we have done wrong. Tell us what we must do to bring back the rain.'

For three days, the people watched. For three days, the people waited. But though winter was over and the sleet moon rose, no rains came.

'Tonight, the wisest of the Elders will go to the high hilltop,' She Who Is Alone told her doll. 'He will hear the words of the Great Spirit. Then we will know what to do to make the rains return.'

'The sun is rising,' called the crier as he ran through the circle of tepees the next morning. 'The Elder is returning.'

The people gathered in a great circle. The Tribal Elder lit the sacred pipe. He drew in a breath of smoke. He blew out a breath of prayer, an offering to the Great Spirit. The Elder offered the pipe to the Four Directions, to the West, to the North, to the East and to the South.

He offered the pipe to Mother Earth and Father Sky.

Then he spoke. 'The Great Spirit has sent me a vision,' he said. 'Our people have been careless. We have taken and taken from Mother Earth but we have given nothing in return. This drought is a warning.'

The people listened.

'We must give something back. An offering to the Great Spirit. Our most precious possession. We must burn it and scatter the ashes to the Four Winds. Only then will the rains return.'

So a great fire was built.

'What will you give to heal your land and save your people?' the Elder asked. People looked around, each waiting for someone else to speak. But no one spoke. People looked at the ground. A warrior shifted his weight from foot to foot. A woman fingered her beaded moccasins. An old man examined the edge of his blanket.

At last the brittle silence was broken. 'Surely it is not my bow the Great Spirit wants,' said the young man. 'I must hunt to find food so that we may eat.'

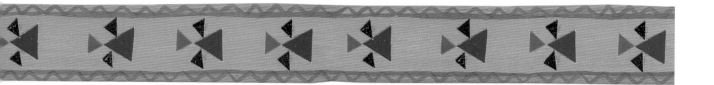

The old man clutched his blanket tightly around his shoulders. 'And I will freeze to death without this.'

'Not my moccasins,' pleaded the young woman. 'They are too beautiful to burn.'

The sun set and still there were no offers. People drifted away to the warmth of their lodges. Tepee flaps closed.

She Who Is Alone lay in her tepee listening to the chirr of the nightjar and the distant howl of the coyote. What could she, a young girl, do for the Great Spirit? What could she give?

She felt the familiar weight of her doll in her hand, its warmth against her cheek.

She looked down at her doll. 'You,' she said softly. 'You are my most precious possession.'

And she knew what she had to do.

She Who Is Alone slipped from her sleeping furs and out into the solemn night. Clutching her doll, she crept to the embers of the great fire. A single stick glowed. Carefully, quietly, she lifted it out. Holding the ember above her, and clutching her precious, precious doll, she climbed the sacred rock.

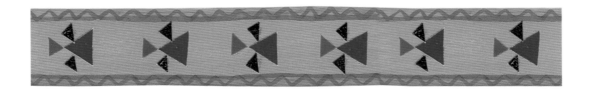

She walked until her home was far behind and the plains were far below. A million stars lit her way.

There, on the hilltop, she gathered twigs and kindled a flame. On her knees, she blew her breath into the heart of the fire. She watched the twigs begin to catch and spark. The fire leapt to life.

'Oh, Great Spirit,' She Who Is Alone began. Her voice was small in the vastness of the night. 'Please help me to be brave. All I have in the world is my doll. She is the most precious thing I can give.'

Alone on the hilltop, where sky and earth touch, the girl sat. With a quiet heart, she listened.

She listened to the poetry of the moon.

She listened to the stories of the stones.

She watched the stars dancing.

There, alone on top of the world, she felt how all beings are related, all one family. And she did not feel alone.

The little girl hugged and hugged her doll. She buried her face in the softness of it. She inhaled the scent of her mother.

She thought about her people — how they had cared for her, how they were suffering. She Who Is Alone looked up, her eyes full of tears and stars.

'Oh, Great Spirit,' she prayed, 'please accept my gift and send us rain again.'

Her throat ached. She couldn't speak to say goodbye. She held out her doll and laid it down in the flames.

She Who Is Alone watched as the fire accepted her offering. She watched the smoke curling, coiling, up and away. She hugged her knees and watched until her doll was no more than a faint ember, glowing.

Then she took a handful of cold, white ash and scattered it to the Four Winds.

Exhausted, she fell asleep.

First light woke her. Rubbing the sleep from her eyes, she looked down the hill.

Stretching out in all directions was a sea of flowers. Blue flowers, butterfly blue.

The whole camp gathered on the hill with She Who Is Alone, gazing at the miracle.

The air tingled. She Who Is Alone could taste it. Thunder. *Drip.* A raindrop. *Drip.* Another. *Drip, drip.* The skies opened and the life-giving rains came at last.

She Who Is Alone lifted her face to the sky. The gentle rain washed away her tears. And so the rain returned, a quiet blessing, and the land began to heal.

A great ceremony was held, and She Who Is Alone was given a new name. The Tribal Elder called it out. He called it to the East, to the South,

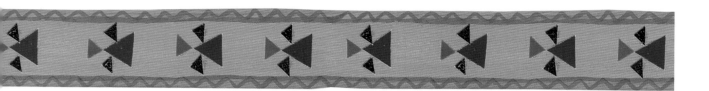

to the West and to the North. He called out her name to the sky and to the earth. He called out her name to the plants and to the animals. He called out her name: 'She Who Loved Her People'.

And from that day onwards, every new spring moon, the Great Spirit remembers the gift of the little girl and fills the hills and valleys of the land with flowers. Blue flowers, butterfly blue.

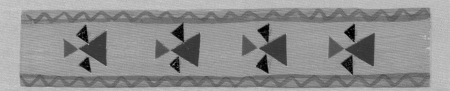

# Make a cornhusk doll

Native peoples make dolls from a variety of materials. Comanche dolls are often made from buckskin. Many native peoples of northeastern America make dolls from cornhusks. Use your leftover cornhusks to make your own doll.

You will need:
- Cornhusks (the green outer layer of fresh corn on the cob, or use dry husks and soak them in water first to soften them)
- String
- Scissors

**Step 1:** Make the head and body: fold a cornhusk in half, and tie a knot with string 2.5cm (1in) below the fold. Now you have your doll's head and body.

**Step 2:** Make the arms: roll another husk lengthwise, to make a long tube. This will be your doll's arms. Tie the arms about 1cm ($^1/_2$in) from the ends to make wrists and hands.

**Step 3:** To attach the arms, slide the arm section up the centre of the body. Tie a piece of string tightly below the arms to hold them in place and make a waist. You now have a cornhusk doll with a cornhusk skirt.

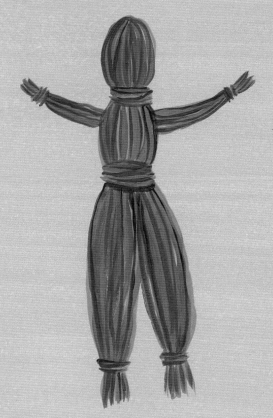

**Step 4:** If you want your doll to have trouser legs instead of a skirt, cut the skirt in two, almost to the waist tie. Then tie each leg about 2.5cm (1in) from the bottom to make ankles.

# Bali

This is a traditional tale from Bali, an island in Indonesia. Surrounded by reefs, with a landscape of white-sand beaches, rain forest jungles, lush rice terraces and volcanic mountain peaks, Bali is famous for its tropical beauty. The tale reflects the understanding that everything in nature is connected in one way or another.

Today, our daily lives can often feel disconnected from the rest of the world. We don't see where our food is grown, how our clothes are made or where our rubbish ends up. This story shows us that, although we may see only part of the web, all things are woven together. And it reminds us that one person's actions affect the whole web of life.

45

# Grumpy Gecko

## BALI

PURRRR… In a shady glade, the chief of the jungle slept. Until, GECK-O! GECK-O! GECK-O!

Tiger woke up with a snort. He opened one round yellow eye. 'Gecko,' he growled. 'What do you want? It's the middle of the night.'

'I've come to complain…'

Tiger narrowed his eyes. What could Gecko the lizard have to complain about? He spent most of his time lazing around, just sleeping and eating. Even when he was hungry, all he had to do was flick out his sticky tongue and lick up a mosquito.

'What's troubling you?' Tiger asked.

'It's the fireflies!' said Gecko. 'All night long they fly around, flashing their lights in my eyes, keeping me awake. Hour after hour, night after night, flashing and flickering…I haven't slept for days.' Gecko rolled out his long tongue and licked his eyeball. 'It's making me very grumpy.'

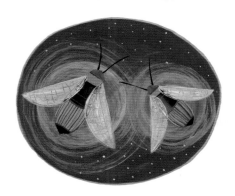

'Yes, Gecko,' Tiger yawned. 'I can imagine.'

'Well,' said Gecko, 'you're the chief of the jungle. Go and talk to them about it. Make them stop.'

Tiger stifled another gigantic yawn. 'I'll talk to the fireflies,' he promised Gecko.

Gecko scuttled off into the night, muttering to himself, 'All night long, flashing and flickering, flickering and flashing…'

Tiger sighed and set off to find the fireflies.

Wading through wet paddy fields, Tiger's great paws sent the silver reflections of stars rippling across the water. The night vibrated with the chirps and croaks of frogs and the trills of a million insects.

Above the paddies, the fireflies flickered and flashed.

'Fireflies,' Tiger called, 'Gecko says you have been disturbing his sleep, flashing and flickering all night long. Is this true?'

'Ooooh! It's Tiger!' giggled the fireflies, fluttering and flashing more than ever. 'The chief of the jungle himself.'

Tiger coughed. 'Fireflies, please. I just want to know why you have been disturbing Gecko.'

'Well, we do flash our lights all night,' replied the fireflies, 'but we don't want to disturb anyone! We're just passing on Woodpecker's message. We heard him drumming out a warning.'

'I see,' said Tiger. 'Then I'll talk to Woodpecker.'

At the edge of the paddies, Tiger found Woodpecker drumming against a coconut palm. *Rat-a-tat, rat-a-tat, rat-a-tat.*

'Woodpecker!' Tiger winced. 'Woodpecker, please explain this incessant tapping!'

'What?' Woodpecker stopped hammering for a moment and Tiger opened his eyes.

'The fireflies say you have been rapping and tapping, tapping and rapping, drumming out a warning. Is this true?'

'Of course,' said Woodpecker, puffing up his feathers. 'I provide a great service. Clearly, my efforts are not appreciated.' He looked down his long beak at Tiger. 'Beetle rolls manure right across the path. I warn the jungle animals so that no one steps in it. Without my drumming, who knows what a mess you'd all be in?'

'Oh,' said Tiger. 'Well, that's very helpful. Thank you.'

Tiger licked his nose thoughtfully. 'I'll go and speak to Beetle.'

It was easy to spot Beetle on the jungle path. In the moonlight, his back gleamed like polished metal.

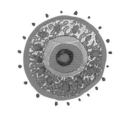

'What's all this?' Tiger asked. 'Woodpecker says you're rolling filthy mess all over the place?'

'Yes, yes, can't stop,' Beetle replied, rolling a ball of dung right up to Tiger's paw. 'Water Buffalo drops piles of it all over the path. If I don't move some away, there'll be muck everywhere! 'Scuse me…'

Tiger lifted his paw and Beetle bustled past.

'OK,' said Tiger, suppressing a sigh. 'Thank you, Beetle. I'll go and see Buffalo.'

Tiger found Buffalo asleep in a pool of mud.

'Buffalo,' Tiger roared.

Spluttering and blinking, Buffalo clambered out of his wallow.

He gulped. 'Yes, Sir?'

'Beetle says you have been leaving your manure all over the path. Is this true?'

'Oh yes, Sir,' said Buffalo, lowering his head. 'I leave manure all over the path, Sir. But you see, Sir, it's helpful, Sir. Rain washes holes in the path every afternoon. I leave manure only to fill up the holes, so that no one trips or falls. If I didn't, Sir, someone could get hurt.'

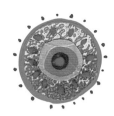

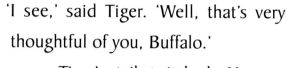

'I see,' said Tiger. 'Well, that's very thoughtful of you, Buffalo.'

Tiger's tail twitched. He was beginning to lose patience. He sighed. 'I'll go and hear what Rain has to say.'

Tiger set off for Mount Agung, the highest peak on the island, and the home of Rain.

Tiger climbed and he climbed and he climbed.

He climbed through humid jungle hung with vines and strung with flowers.

He climbed through open woodland where cool air currents made his whiskers quiver.

He scrambled through scrub and stumbled over loose stones.

At last, his claws clattered onto the smooth grass of the mountain peak. He stopped to catch his breath. He looked down the mountain.

The sun was rising. Tiger stared.

Jungle spread out for miles around, flamboyant with flowers. Wild orchids and climbing lilies, trumpets of violet-blue and starbursts of brilliant flame-red.

Tiger sniffed. He smelt jasmine, ylang-ylang, frangipani.

He swivelled his ears. He heard newborn streams trickling and tinkling.

And below the jungle, on the green-gold steps of the paddy fields, he could just make out the faint flicker and flash of the fireflies.

'No need to ask why Rain rains,' Tiger smiled.

He cooled his paws in a stream and watched for a while. He watched the water journey from mountain to sea, sustaining every living thing on its way, even the tiniest mosquito.

Tiger plunged his muzzle into the clear fresh water and drank.

Then he began the long journey down the mountain and through the forests and jungles and paddies to find Gecko.

It was dusk by the time Tiger found the lizard again.

'Well?' Gecko demanded. 'Did you talk to the fireflies? They're still flashing and flickering, flickering and flashing, on and on and on. Did you tell them to stop?'

'Gecko,' said Tiger. He sat down on his haunches and spoke very slowly. 'Listen carefully. The fireflies flash to pass on Woodpecker's warning. Woodpecker warns everyone not to step in Beetle's dung. Beetle clears up the excess dung left by Buffalo. Buffalo leaves manure on the path to fill up the holes made by Rain. Rain makes holes in the path as he creates streams and lakes and puddles — puddles where mosquitoes live.'

'Oh,' said Gecko.

'Gecko, what do you eat?'

'Mosquitoes,' said Gecko.

'So…' said Tiger.

'So…' repeated Gecko slowly.

'Yes…'

'If Rain stopped raining…'

'Yes…'

'Buffalo could stop filling holes…'

'Uh-huh…'

'And Beetle could stop rolling dung…'

'Yes…'

'And Woodpecker could stop drumming…'

'Mmm…'

'And the fireflies could stop flashing…'

'Yes, Gecko…'

'But…I would have nothing to eat.'

'Exactly,' said Tiger. 'Gecko, everything in this world is connected. Go and live in peace with the fireflies.'

So Gecko stuck himself upside down, underneath a branch of a tree. He closed his eyes. He went to sleep.

The fireflies flickered and flashed.

Tiger snored. *PURRRR…*

53

# Grow your own tomatoes

Plant seeds in the spring to harvest home-grown tomatoes throughout the summer.

**You will need:**

- Tomato seeds
- A seed tray (an old egg box works well)
- Potting organic compost
- A trowel
- A watering can
- Stakes
- Twine

**Step 1:** In early spring, fill your seed tray with potting compost. Sprinkle a few tomato seeds into each section. Lightly cover the seeds with potting compost and give them a little water.

**Step 2:** Place the seed tray in a warm, well-lit place until the seeds begin to sprout (about 7 – 10 days). Keep the soil moist by watering regularly.

**Step 3:** When the seedlings appear, remove the weakest ones from each section so that you are left with just one plant per section. Turn the seed tray around every few days to help the plants grow upright.

**Step 4:** In early summer, move your plants outside to larger pots. To do this, water well, then push up the bottom of each seed-tray section. Ease out the compost and the plant. Fill a pot $^3/_4$ full of compost. You will need one pot per plant. Using a trowel, make a hole in the compost, place the plant into it and fill around the plant with more compost.

**Step 5:** As your plants grow taller they will need support. Put a long, strong stake into the soil next to each plant. Loosely tie the main stem to the stake as it grows. Water the soil regularly to keep it moist.

**Step 6:** When the plant has formed three or four clusters of tomatoes, pinch off the top shoot of the plant. You can also pinch off the side shoots that grow from each leaf joint. This helps the plant's energy go into ripening tomatoes instead of growing more leaves.

**Step 7:** Pick your tomatoes when they are red and ripe. Savour them in salads, sauces and sandwiches...or just eat them straight from the vine!

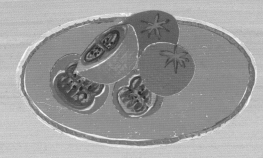

# Kazakhstan

For thousands of years, nomadic tribes roamed the steppes — large flat grasslands — of Central Asia. They travelled hundreds of miles, migrating from high summer pastures to warmer winter lowlands, accompanied by their horses, sheep, cattle, goats and camels. They lived in yurts — portable, dome-shaped tents made from felt.

The word 'kazakh' means 'free man'. Kazakh nomads loved the freedom to wander in their vast land of steppes and mountains ranges.

Below the steppes, in southern Kazakhstan, caravan routes wove through thriving cities.

In the days of the Silk Road, the ancient town of Almaty was an oasis for travellers and traders alike. Today, it is an important commercial and cultural centre. The city remains green with gardens and is famous for its apple trees. Botanists believe this is where the first apple trees took root.

Enclosed gardens, like the one in this tale, are central to Islamic cultures across the world. With flowing waterways and tinkling fountains, bright flowers and fresh fruit, as well as shade and shelter from trees and pavilions, gardens were seen as places of peace, harmony and happiness.

This story celebrates the earthly paradise that is a garden.

# The Magic Garden

## Kazakhstan

In olden times in Kazakhstan, there lived two neighbours. Asan was a farmer. Hassan was a shepherd. They were friends.

One year, the winter was so severe and the land was so frozen that Hassan's sheep could not reach the grass under the ice, and his whole flock perished. Blinking back tears, Hassan went to his friend. 'My flock has all gone,' he told him. 'Without them I cannot survive. So I'm leaving. Goodbye, Asan.'

But Asan would not hear of it. 'Never,' he vowed. 'You shall have half my land and share my farm with me.'

'Asan, you are generous and kind, but I cannot accept,' the shepherd protested. 'Your field is small already. You cannot make it smaller.'

'Nonsense,' insisted the farmer. 'You are my friend and I want you to stay. True, we will have less than

before, but we will have enough. I will not take "no" for an answer.' At this, Hassan's tears overflowed, and he hugged his friend to his chest. So the shepherd stayed.

Days passed and nights passed. Months passed and years passed. One day, Hassan was working his field when *CLUNK!* His hoe struck something hard. An old pot. Hassan heaved it out of the ground and looked inside. His mouth fell open. Gold coins!

'Asan, Asan,' called the old shepherd. 'You are rich! Look!'

The farmer smiled warmly. 'Hassan, how unselfish you are. But this is your gold, not mine. After all, you found it yourself on your own land.'

'You have given me enough already.' Hassan held out the pot. 'Here, take your treasure.'

'Your treasure,' corrected Asan. 'You keep it.'

Asan and Hassan began to argue. For the first time, the two friends could not agree. Finally, they decided to go to the village wise man for help with with their problem.

Inside his yurt, the wise man sat with four students. Bowing low, the visitors explained their problem. The wise man listened. Asan and Hassan waited. And waited. But, for a long time, the wise man sat in silence.

Then he turned, not to Asan nor to Hassan, but to his first student. 'Here is an interesting situation,' he said. 'Tell me, what would you advise?'

The first student answered immediately. 'The solution is obvious. The gold came from the ground. Neither of these men will accept it. So bury the gold in the ground again.'

The wise man frowned. He turned to his second student. 'And what do you suggest?'

The second student answered, 'The gold was brought to you. I think you should keep it yourself.'

The wise man raised his eyebrows. 'Indeed.' He turned to his third student. 'And what do you say?'

'The gold was found in a field. The field is in the kingdom, and the kingdom belongs to the Khan. Let the Khan keep all of the treasure.'

The wise man's face darkened. 'And you?' he asked the last and youngest student.

The boy, Arman, gave a little shake of his head, as if to blow

away a daydream. 'Well, I do have one idea…' he hesitated. 'If I were to choose what to do with the gold, I would buy seeds. Then we could plant a garden…' And, with shining eyes, he described his vision. He spoke of a beautiful garden where people could rest and play, birds and animals could make their homes, wildflowers could flourish, and bees and butterflies could thrive.

The wise man was listening with eyes closed. Now he laid his hand on the boy's arm. 'Your decision is wise.' He turned to the two men. 'Do you agree?'

Asan and Hassan looked at each other and nodded. 'Yes, yes, a garden; let there be a garden…'

So the wise man instructed his disciple, 'Go to the capital, and with this gold, buy the finest seeds you can find. Then, on the steppes, plant the garden of your dreams.'

And so the student set off, overjoyed at his good luck. For many days, Arman travelled the dry and dusty trail, until he came to the royal city. But oh! What a hubbub! The noise! The colour! On every side,

61

merchants called, selling strange and wonderful wares. The din of a dozen languages made his head buzz. Pungent incense made his nose tickle and his eyes prickle. At last, he stumbled and bumped his way to the seller of seeds. As he fingered the precious kernels, a piteous crying made him spin around. Crossing the square was a caravan strung with birds of every kind. There were thousands of them. And they were alive. The birds' feet were tied and their wings were crusted with dust. With every lurching movement of the caravan, the birds' heads banged against the camels' sides.

Arman couldn't stand it. Without a second thought, he confronted the caravan leader. 'What are you doing with these birds?' he demanded.

'These birds are for the table of the Khan,' the camel driver answered. 'He will feast on their meat and decorate his palace with their feathers. I have here birds caught in the deserts, steppes and mountains, birds trapped in woodlands, marshes and lakes. I have here the rarest birds in the whole kingdom. Some of them are the last of their kind!' Arman could not believe the pride in the man's voice.

'I will give you gold,' said Arman, 'if you let these birds go.' The man laughed and began to lead his camels away.

'No, look!' Arman opened his bag, revealing the treasure. The camel driver's eyes widened — this was more than even the Khan would pay.

He snatched the bag quickly, before the boy could change his mind.

Arman began untying the birds. The stronger birds stretched their wings and soared into the sky. But some were too weak to fly. These Arman placed carefully on the ground. When all the birds were free, he picked up an injured starling. He warmed it in his hands. Then, using a single finger, he massaged gently, gently, around the bird's head. Now the bird sat quietly on his open palm. It looked around and flew away.

It took Arman the whole day, but with each one that took to the sky, his heart was a little lighter. Then at last he dusted off his knees and turned for home. He felt warm, as though he were glowing, and his feet skipped along.

But as he neared home, his feet seemed to grow heavier and heavier. You fool, Arman, he thought to himself. That gold was meant to buy seeds. What would he say to his master? And to the kind-hearted neighbours? It was their money. They had trusted him with it. And he had lost it all.

'And now there will be no garden,' he said aloud. And with that thought, he slumped to the ground and wept.

Nearby, a starling cocked its head, listening. Then it flew away.

What was that noise? Looking up, Arman found the air rushing with wings and brilliant with feathers. Bird after bird glided down to him. 'You saved our lives,' sang the birds, 'now let us help you.'

The boy looked around in astonishment. The whole vast steppe was busy with birds, scratching the earth and pecking the ground — preparing the land for planting. Falcons alighted from distant lands, their beaks full of exotic seeds. Using wing and beak and claw, the birds planted the seeds. With powerful talons, eagles dug out ponds, and pelicans brought water to fill them.

For a long time, Arman sat entranced. When he stood up, the birds rushed into the sky as one. And now, what magic was this? The seeds were sprouting. Before he could blink, stalks grew into trees and blossomed. Before he could think, the blossoms fell, and there grew apples as round and shiny as gold coins.

The grass swayed with poppies and tulips. Petal-strewn paths wove between tranquil pools. A thousand birds were singing.

Arman stared. Was he dreaming? To be sure, he plucked a golden apple and ran with it back to the wise man's yurt.

'Arman!' The wise man opened his arms wide and embraced his student. Bright-eyed and breathless, Arman poured out his adventures and held out the golden fruit.

The wise man crunched into the apple. Its sweet juice filled his mouth and he knew that the golden treasure had been transformed.

Shining with happiness, Arman led the wise man, Asan and Hassan to the garden.

Soon the people of the steppes arrived. Asan and Hassan watched them stroll beneath the trees. The old friends looked at each other and grinned.

People young and old rested and played. The fresh fruit and clean water nourished their bodies. The cool shade and soft lawns rested their minds. And the sound of a thousand birds singing sent their spirits soaring.

Such is the story of the magic garden, which grew from the generosity of two old friends and the dream of one young boy.

# Make a pine cone birdfeeder

Keep the birds in your garden happy and healthy with this easy-to-make feeder.

**You will need:**

- One large, open pine cone
- String
- Lard
- Oats
- Birdseed
- A shallow dish

**Step 1**: Loop the string under the top scales of the pine cone and tie it in a tight knot.

**Step 2**: Mix the lard and the oats together in a bowl.

**Step 3**: Push the mixture into the pine cone, filling the spaces between the scales. Spread the mixture all over the surface of the pine cone.

**Step 4**: Pour some birdseed into the shallow dish.

**Step 5**: Roll the pine cone in the birdseed until it is well covered.

**Step 6**: Hang the pine cone feeder in your garden for the birds to enjoy.

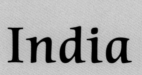

# India

This folk tale, from the Bishnoi tribes of India, is based on a true story. The events took place in 1730 in the village now known as Khejarli. The village is named after the khejari tree: Amrita's tree.

In the arid regions of Rajasthan, the Bishnoi tribes practise a faith based on reverence for nature. They eat a vegetarian diet and protect local wildlife, allowing wild birds and animals to graze on their crops and drink at their water tanks.

Their religion forbids the cutting of any green tree; carpenters will wait for a tree to die naturally before harvesting timber. Bishnoi people of all ages help to plant and look after sacred forest groves, called 'orans'.

Because of their conservation efforts and attention to ecological balance, the Thar Desert in Rajasthan is the greenest desert on the planet. It supports more human and animal populations than any other.

The following folk tale inspired the Chipko ('Hug the Trees') Movement, whose members embrace trees to prevent forests from being felled. Chipko activists have saved thousands of trees throughout India. Their successes have inspired conservation efforts worldwide, spreading a message of courage and hope.

Many believe that Bishnoi ideas of peaceful resistance, based on the events at Khejarli, influenced Mahatma Gandhi himself.

# Amrita's Tree

## INDIA

Amrita leaned back against her favourite tree and rested. After the glare of the desert sun, it was cool and green in the forest grove.

Sometimes, Amrita climbed her tree. Sometimes the wind swayed her and she was a forest queen. Sometimes she talked to her tree, sharing her daydreams and her secrets, but today was so peaceful that she sat in silence.

The forest was drowsy with sun and hazy with light. Amrita gazed up at the glowing green leaves, the shifting shapes of sun and shade. Even the wind seemed hushed.

A peacock rested. Black bucks grazed. Rabbits

hopped about unafraid. A leaf spiralled lazily to the ground. Amrita closed her eyes and sighed with pleasure.

*CAAWK!* She heard an unearthly shriek, the shrill alarm call of the peacock, echoing through the forest. A shiver shot down Amrita's spine and she scrambled to her feet.

With a flick of their tails, the gazelles were gone. The rabbits scattered. Now Amrita heard the tramp of many heavy boots, the crack of branches snapping. Through the trees she saw men marching, each one carrying something. Amrita strained to see. Bright edges! Sharp flashes! They were carrying axes.

'Cut down every tree you can,' she heard the chief woodcutter say. 'The Maharajah needs plenty of wood…' Amrita drew in her breath. They couldn't cut down the forest! Without these trees there'd be no fruit to eat, no leaves to feed the cows, no shelter from the sun.

Above her, watching over her, Amrita's own tree stirred in the breeze. 'I won't let them hurt you,' she said out loud. 'I promise I'll protect you. I don't know how, but I will!'

Quick as a black buck, she ran. In the village, she could hear the slap and slop of the butter churn and the soft *clap, clap, clap* of chapattis being patted into shape. The women were busy. Amrita found her mother. 'Amma, Amma,' she panted, pushing windswept hair out of her eyes, 'I saw men in the forest, men with axes, and they are going to cut down the trees!'

Amrita's mother got up so quickly that she knocked over her water pot. But she did not stop to right it. Amrita's mother rushed around the village, calling the women away from their work. 'We must save the trees!' She urged. 'Come on!'

Had the men looked up from ploughing the fields at that moment, they would have seen a breathtaking procession of women and children, wives and daughters, grandmothers and babies bouncing on backs. All of them hurrying towards the forest, their saris swirling behind them in swathes of saffron and scarlet, their mirrored tops spangling, their bracelets and anklets jangling.

They arrived to find the woodcutters sharpening their axes. Amrita's mother greeted the men politely, pressing her hands together and bowing her head: 'Namaste. We do not want trouble, but we cannot let you cut down these trees.'

The chief woodcutter cast his eyes over the straggle of women before him — as colourful as desert flowers in their vibrant saris, and just as helpless. He snorted. 'You do not own these trees. We have orders from the Maharajah of Jodhpur.'

'Sir, these trees are our life,' Amrita's mother implored. 'Their roots hold the soil together; they keep the land from sliding away during the monsoon rains. Without them our fields and homes will be washed away.'

'Never mind your mud huts,' the chief replied with a sweep of his hand. 'With this timber the Maharajah will have the finest palace in all of India!'

'Please!' begged Amrita's mother. 'These roots soak up rain, so the earth can give us spring water. Can't you see? We need these trees to survive.'

'Enough!' barked the chief. 'What do I care about your precious water? These trees have already been marked for felling.'

Amrita's aunt often came to the forest to gather herbs to make medicines. She tried to reason with the chief. 'Sir, see how rich this is.' She crumbled a handful of earth. 'It is nourished by fallen leaves. If you take these trees, the plants, the herbs, everything growing here will die. Think of the cures for countless illnesses…'

The chief scowled. 'We've heard enough. Now, out of my way and let me work.' And he pushed the old woman roughly aside so that she stumbled and fell. Amrita felt the heat rush to her face as she helped her aunt to her feet. This woman had saved her brother's life when he was sick last winter. Had these men no shame?

'Now!' ordered the chief. 'Cut down the trees!' A burly woodcutter shouldered his axe and strolled over to an ancient khejari. With a swift swoop his iron blade bit deep into the bark.

*Hack, hack, hack*, he hacked so hard that the whole grove shuddered. *Hack, hack, hack*, flecks of red tree-sap stained his shirt. *Hack, hack, CRACK!* With a terrible groan the mighty tree came crashing to the ground. Amrita's mother covered her mouth with her hands. Amrita stared in disbelief.

'Stop!' someone cried. But the men did not stop. The woodcutters began to chop at another tree, and another. Soon the grove was a graveyard of trees. Broken limbs scattered the floor. Leaves dropped like tears.

A woodcutter brushed past Amrita, towards her own special tree. 'No! No! Please don't!' she cried, tears springing to her eyes. 'Please don't cut down my tree.' The woodcutter advanced.

The sharp tang of bleeding trunks was stinging Amrita's nostrils and tears were stinging her eyes. Amrita stepped in front of him, blocking his path. Her voice shook as she spoke: 'I will not let anyone harm my tree.'

The woodcutter laughed out loud. 'Little girl, there's nothing you can do to stop us.' Amrita thought of her beloved tree lying dead on the forest floor.

She thought of never again dreaming beneath its branches. Never again swaying in the treetops. And she ran from the woodcutter towards her tree.

'Amrita, stop! Come back! Amrita!'

Amrita ignored her mother's cries and flung her arms around her tree, pressing herself against it. 'If you want to cut the tree, you will have to cut me first!' The man and his axe were behind her. She could hear the sound of her own breathing, hard and loud and fast. The man raised his sharp blade.

'Swing your axe!' commanded the chief. Amrita clenched her teeth and clung onto her old friend, so that the bumpy bark was pressing into her cheek and arms. She looked up, up, up — to the sturdy trunk reaching to the sky, to the branches sheltering her like loving arms. She felt the roots under her feet, anchoring her deep down into the earth.

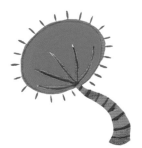

She felt the strength of the tree coursing through her. And she knew with a fierce bright certainty that she was doing the right thing.

'Swing your axe!' the chief shouted again.

'I…' the woodcutter faltered. He looked down at the girl — this mere sapling of a girl — her eyes squeezed shut, her thin arms hugging so tight, her tear-stained cheeks pale with fright. 'I…I cannot.'

Amrita opened one eye, then another, to see the woodcutter's head bowed, his axe at his feet. All around her, people were hugging trees. Women and children, wives and daughters, grandmothers and toddlers all hugged the trees. Some ancient trees had trunks so broad that generations of women were joining hands to embrace them.

The axes lay on the forest floor. The men huddled together and talked in low voices. Then, without a word, the labourers picked up their axes and walked out of the wood.

'What were you thinking of?' Amrita's mother called. 'I was so afraid.'

'So was I,' said Amrita. She clung to her tree and kissed it, over and over again.

Later, in the darkening dusk, Amrita leaned back against her tree and rested. Pigeons cooed quietly. A peacock flapped into the branches to roost. Amrita sighed with pleasure.

'Amrita…' She heard her mother call.

Her mother sat down beside Amrita on the forest floor and stroked

her hair. 'You know the woodcutters will tell the Maharajah what happened,' she said gently. 'They will come back, or the Maharajah himself will come…'

Tucking a stray lock of hair behind her daughter's ear, her mother smiled. 'You are just like your tree,' she said. 'Strong inside, like heartwood.' Amrita smiled at her mother, and arm in arm they walked back home.

The next morning, the women were distracted at their work. Their hands were busy, but their eyes strayed to the horizon. Would the woodcutters return? Or the Maharajah? Would he punish those who had dared to defy his orders?

That afternoon, in a thunder of hooves and a cloud of dust, the Maharajah arrived.

The women joined hands and pulled their children close. Amrita's mother bit her lip. But Amrita rose to greet the Maharajah with all the dignity of a forest queen.

She was surprised to see that he carried not an axe but a bright bundle. He climbed down from his horse. Amrita watched in wonder as he unwrapped the silken cloth. Inside was a copper plate, engraved with

a royal decree. 'I present this to you, Amrita,' said the Maharajah, kneeling down on the dusty ground, 'and to the women of your village, in honour of your courage and your wisdom. I promise that, from this day on, no tree in this forest will ever be cut down.'

There were joyous celebrations that night. Flowers and garlands adorned every tree. Waves of music floated through the forest and mingled with delicious smells from the feast. Fireworks lit up the sky.

As Amrita drifted off to sleep, the cheers of the villagers still sang in her ears and the flash of fireworks still sparkled behind her eyelids. She slept with a smile on her lips.

Hundreds of years later, folk songs of the people who hugged the trees still echo through the villages of India. Amrita's courage has inspired people across the land to stand together to protect forests. Thousands of trees have been saved, and a million more planted.

And in one sacred grove, Amrita's tree still grows.

# Build a willow den

Create a leafy hideaway in your garden for you to call your own.

You will need:
- Living willow rods
- A spade
- String
- Extra weaving material: leaves, vines, grass, wool
- A stick

**Step 1**: Use a stick attached to some string to scratch the shape of a circle into the ground.

**Step 2**: Using a spade, dig out the grass from the circumference of the circle. Leave a patch of uncut grass where you want the doorway to be.

**Step 3**: Push your longest willow rods into the cleared ground, about 20cm (8in) deep. Space them evenly around the edge of the circle, leaving a gap on one side for the doorway.

**Step 4**: Tie the tops of the rods together.

**Step 5**: Now weave your smaller rods in and out of the upright rods, working from the bottom up. You could also weave in bits of vine, long leaves, grass or coloured wool. Remember to leave a space for the door. (When you come to the doorway, just bend your weaving material around the upright rod and weave it back the other way.)

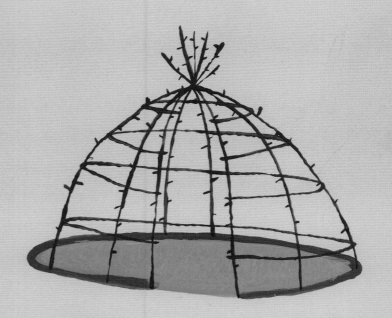

**Step 6**: Give the willow rods some water, then admire your creation and wait for your den to grow!

# Wales

According to Celtic folklore, a large number of nature spirits once peopled Britain: patrons of wildlife, personified forces of nature, and local spirits guarding particular rocks, pools and woods.

The Celtic people of Wales, Ireland and Scotland have a rich tradition of tales and beliefs about fairies. Certain fairies can become invisible, change their shape or fly; some live underground, others in trees or wells or lakes. Their enchanted world is always close to the human world, and it is always wise to treat the fairies with respect.

This fairy tale comes from Wales, a land of meadows and moors, craggy mountains and rolling valleys, surrounded on three sides by the sea.

This story shows us that habitats are all around us, even if we can't see them. It illustrates the impact of our waste on these fragile environments, reminding us to be considerate neighbours.

85

# Stink Water

## WALES

The old man and the old woman lived in a little whitewashed cottage in the hills.

Every evening, the old woman made supper. While the stew was bubbling on the stove, she'd clean the peelings into a bucket. Soggy sprout tops, slimy leek skins and slippery twists of potato peel.

She'd scoop up the sludgy stuff and into the bucket it went. *SLOP!*

She'd squeeze together the squishy bits and into the bucket they went. *SQUELCH!*

She'd sponge off the splatters and splotches of goodness knows what, and into the bucket they went. *SPLOT!*

After their vegetable stew, she'd wash the dishes and into the bucket went the dirty dishwater. *SWISH!*

Then, carefully, carefully, the old man would stagger with the sloshy-splashy bucket out the front door. Step, step, rest. Step, step, rest. Step, step, *SPLOSH!* He'd dump the overflowing bucket over the garden wall.

One evening, as dusk settled on the fields, the old man rested for a moment. He wasn't getting any younger, or the bucket any lighter. He straightened up stiffly and rubbed the small of his back.

'So it's you!' squeaked a voice.

'What?' The old man peered through the fading light.

'Down here! I said: It's you — pouring your filthy stink water over the wall!' It was a teeny tiny fairy with a wrinkly ruddy face like an old rosehip.

The old man rubbed his eyes. 'Yes,' he said, 'I do — every evening.'

'I know!' The fairy gave a deep sigh.

'But what harm does it do?' asked the old man.

At this, the fairy started up such a sighing and a moaning and a groaning that it made the old man's heart ache. 'Whatever is the matter?'

'Look closely,' the fairy said. 'And you'll see…'

'Stars of mine!' exclaimed the old man. There, on just the other side of the wall, was a teeny tiny cottage. But what a mess!

Curls of crusty stuff were caked around the chimney. Roof slates were sticky with squishy bits. And the well was all sour with stink water.

'Right down my chimney it comes!' complained the fairy, and his face crumpled as if he were about to cry.

Out of the little house came the fairy's wife. In the crook of her arm nestled a tiny bundle, a baby. Pale and pinched he looked, and he was quiet as the grave.

'Our child is sick,' the fairy wife said. 'If he doesn't have clean water to drink soon…' She buried her face in her husband's shoulder.

The old man was horrified. 'But this is terrible!' he cried. 'We had no idea… But I don't know what we can do. We need to get rid of our rubbish, and what with the bucket being so heavy, I can't manage carrying it further than the wall. I'm not as young as I used to be.'

Seeing the look the fairy couple gave him, the old man thought his heart might break, so he added, 'Well, wait a moment, let me think…'

The fairy wife took the babe indoors, and the fairy and the old man sat down together to think. Well, they sat there staring and sighing until the moon had risen, but they couldn't think of a single solution.

'Here's what I'll do,' announced the fairy, 'I'll come back in three days' time. Perhaps by then you will have thought of something.' And with that, they said goodnight.

'What on earth has kept you out so long?' asked the old woman.

The old man told his wife the whole tale, all about the fairy fellow and the tiny cottage and the stink water and everything.

'Oh, but those poor people!' said the old woman. 'That little baby.' And she twisted her shawl in her hands.

Next day, from dawn to twilight, the old man and the old woman thought and thought.

Come evening, the slop bucket still sat in the corner of the cottage, slimy and stinking.

The old man sat on the doorstep, gazing into the twilight.

'What are you doing out in the damp and the dark, with your old bones?' called his wife. 'Come inside.' And she put her arm around his shoulders to lead him into the bright warmth.

As they turned, an owl swung out of the blue. Low, slow, ghost white. Its sudden screech sent a field mouse scurrying for safety.

'That's it!' cried the old man, 'we'll shout a warning. Before we empty the bucket, we'll call "mind out!" Then the good folk can move out of the way and they won't be splashed with slops.'

The old woman considered this. She shook her head.

'Nay, they can't very well move their home, can they? Nor their well?'

'I suppose not.' The old man's shoulders drooped. And they both went to bed feeling very down-hearted.

Next day, they talked and talked about what to do.

In the evening, the old man sat by the hearth. He thought of the fairy couple sitting in their cottage all dank and damp and dirty.

He stared into the fire, pondering, wondering.

He listened to the crackle and hiss and spit. He watched tongues of fire, leaping and licking.

And he leapt to his feet. 'I know!' His face glowed in the firelight. 'We'll burn our rubbish! We'll set up a big old bonfire every evening.'

The old woman considered this. She shook her head.

'And choke those good people in pothers of filthy smoke? And then we'd still have the ash to get rid of.'

'I suppose so.' The old man's face fell.

And the slop bucket still festered in the corner, stinking and steaming.

On the third day, they thought and they thought all day of ways to help the fairies. But they still couldn't think of a thing.

Until, as the old woman was busy peeling the potatoes and chopping the cabbage and slicing the carrots, an idea came to her.

She pointed her kitchen knife at the wall. 'You know,' she said, 'if we made a back door into our house, you could take the bucket out to the back wall, where our slops won't bother that poor family.'

'And isn't it Farmer Jones' land out back?' she continued. 'I bet his pig would enjoy our scraps, too!'

'What a good idea,' the old man replied, 'but I'm too old now to do a job like that.'

'We could pay the joiner and the mason to do the job for us…'

The old man gave a sad smile. 'With what, my love? Potato peelings?'

'I have a bit of money saved up,' said the old woman. 'I'd like to spend it to help our neighbours.'

At this, the old man hugged his wife fiercely. 'What a wife you are!' he declared. 'What a woman!'

So the old man went out with a spring in his step to greet the fairy that third night.

'Well?' asked the fairy, without a shred of hope in his voice.

'Well, indeed!' replied the old man, and he told the fairy their plan.

'You'd do that for us?' asked the fairy, and he grinned from pointy ear to pointy ear.

So the door was cut.

And that evening, when the stew was bubbling on the stove, the old

woman cleaned her peelings into the bucket.

She scooped up the sludgy stuff and into the bucket it went. *SLOP!*

She squeezed together the squishy bits and into the bucket they went. *SQUELCH!*

She sponged off the splatters and splotches of goodness knows what, and into the bucket they went. *SPLOT!*

She washed the dishes and into the bucket went the dirty water. *SWISH!*

Then, carefully, carefully, the old man staggered the sloshy-splashy bucket out the back door. Step, step, rest. Step, step, rest. Step, step, *SPLOSH!* Over the back wall.

And *SNORT! SNORT!* The farmer's pig ate every last bit.

And every evening, after their good vegetable stew, the old couple would sit by the hearth with the kettle singing on the fire. And in the tiny cottage next door, it was just as clean and cosy. The fairy couple sat together, while their baby lay in his cradle, round and rosy, and content.

# Make a mini water garden

Create a habitat that all kinds of wildlife — fish, newts, snails, dragonflies, butterflies and birds — can thrive in.

You will need:
- A watertight container (ceramic, metal or plastic)
- Pebbles and stones
- Water
- Waterweeds (ask your garden centre for native, not exotic, weeds)
- Plant pots
- Gravel
- Water plants (native, not exotic)

**Step 1:** Find a sunny, sheltered spot for your container, away from any overhanging trees.

**Step 2:** Cover the bottom of the container with a layer of pebbles. Then stack up your largest, flattest stones to create a slope that will stick out of the water. This step will allow creatures such as frogs to climb in and out. It will also attract birds, butterflies and dragonflies to rest on the rocks to drink.

**Step 3:** Fill the container with water. Ideally, use rainwater.

**Step 4:** Add some waterweeds. These grow under the surface and help keep the water clear as well as provide oxygen for aquatic creatures to breathe. Waterweed is sold in bunches without roots. Just push these into a small pot of gravel to keep them in place, then lower them into the water.

**Step 5:** Add water plants. A dwarf water lily is ideal for a small water garden. Simply place the pot at the bottom of the container. The stem will grow until leaves and lily flowers float on the surface.

**Step 6:** Your water garden can provide a home for frogs, newts, dragonflies and countless water creatures. It also gives birds a place to bathe. Sit back and watch the wildlife enjoy your oasis.

## Sources and Acknowledgements

### THE SUN MOTHER – Australia

'The Sun Mother' is based on 'The Story of the Creation' by William Ramsay Smith in *Myths and Legends of the Australian Aboriginals* (George G. Harrap, 1930). The tales in this book were collected by David Unaipon, a Ngarrindjeri writer from the lower Murray River region of Australia. You can learn more about him and read his words in *Legendary Tales of the Australian Aborigines* (The Miegunyah Press, 2006).

### WHY THE SKY IS FAR AWAY – Nigeria

I first heard this tale told orally at a wonderful storytelling weekend run by teacher and teller Sue Hollingsworth. The bare bones of the story can be found in Ulli Beier's *The Origin of Life and Death: African Creation Myths* (Heinemann Educational Books, 1966).

### SHE WHO IS ALONE – American Southwest

I came across this story in *The Legend of the Bluebonnet* by Tomie DePaola (G. P. Putnam's Sons, 1983). The tale is recommended for its active heroine by Nancy Schimmel in her excellent sourcebook *Just Enough to Make a Story* (Sisters' Choice, 1992). If you are interested in reading a wider selection of tales representing the Southwest, woodlands and desert, I recommend *American Indian Myths and Legends*, selected and edited by Richard Erdoes and Alfonso Ortiz (Pantheon Books, 1984).

### GRUMPY GECKO – Bali

'Gecko's Complaint' can be found in *Folk Tales from Bali and Lombok* by Margaret Muth Alibasah (Djambatan English Library, 1990). In Alibasah's retelling, the village chief is a human. Other versions of this folk tale depict the chief as an animal. In Ann Martin Bowler's retelling, *Gecko's Complaint* (Periplus Editions, 2003), he is a lion. I chose to make him a tiger, since Balinese tigers were the only mammals endemic to the island. (This means they originally came from Bali. Many animals living in Bali come from the nearby islands of Java and Sumatra.) The last Balinese tiger was killed by hunters in 1937. The Balinese tiger was one of three subspecies of tiger found in Indonesia. In the 1980s, the Javan tiger was also made extinct, by deforestation and hunting. The Sumatran tiger is severely endangered.

### THE MAGIC GARDEN – Kazakhstan

This folk tale comes from Mary Lou Masey's *Stories of the Steppes* (David McKay Company, 1968). A version also appears in M. R. MacDonald's *Earth Care: World Folktales to Talk About* (Linnet Books, 1999), a superb collection of ecological tales for storytellers.

### AMRITA'S TREE – India

In 1730, Amrita Devi and several hundred villagers sacrificed their lives to protect their forest. The Maharajah of Jodhpur commemorated their courage by forbidding woodcutting in the area. The law is still valid today. An account of these events can be found in *Paving the Way for Peace: Living Philosophies of Bishnois and Jains* by Herma Brockmann and Renato Pichler (Originals, 2001).

In 1974, a young girl spotted woodcutters marching towards Reni forest and alerted villagers. Twenty-seven women and children guarded the trees and the forest was saved. The story spread all over India. As a result, the government banned all tree felling in an area of more than 450 square miles. An account of these events can be found in *Hugging the Trees: The Story of the Chipko Movement* by Thomas Weber (Viking, 1987).

'Amrita's Tree' draws on both these historic events.

### STINK WATER – Wales

Versions of this tale can be found in *The Welsh Fairy Book* by W. Jenkyn Thomas (Fisher Unwin, 1907), *Welsh Legendary Tales* by Elisabeth Sheppard-Jones (Thomas Nelson, 1959) and *Fairy Tales from the British Isles* by Amabel Williams-Ellis (Frederick Warne, 1960).